ROSE RED AND THE BEAR PRINCE

ROSE RED AND THE BEAR PRINCE

ADAPTED AND ILLUSTRATED BY DAN ANDREASEN

HARPERCOLLINSPUBLISHERS

Library of Congress Cataloging-in-Publication Data
Andreasen, Dan.
   Rose Red and the bear prince / retold from the Brothers Grimm by
Dan Andreasen.
        p.   cm.
   ". . . adapted from Snow White and Rose Red by the Brothers Grimm" —
T.p. verso
   Summary: A retelling of the fairy tale in which a young girl saves a bear
from a dwarf's wicked spell.
   ISBN 0-06-027966-4. — ISBN 0-06-027967-2 (lib. bdg.)
   [1. Fairy tales.   2. Folklore—Germany.]   I. Grimm, Jacob, 1785–1863.
II. Grimm, Wilhelm, 1786–1859.   III. Schneeweisschen und Rosenrot.
English.   IV. Title.
PZ8.A5615Ro   2000
[398.2"0943'02]—dc21   98-47525
                                                                              CIP
                                                                              AC

Typography by Elynn Cohen
1   2   3   4   5   6   7   8   9   10
❖
First Edition

For Emily, who is filled with
inspiration and enthusiasm

n a cottage deep in the forest there once lived a poor widow and her only child, Rose Red. The widow gave her daughter this name because she was as lovely as the roses on the rosebush that grew near the garden gate, and as sharp as the thorns.

Rose Red grew up bright and happy. Though she had no other children to play with, she was never lonely. There was the forest to explore, and all the forest animals were her friends. Rose Red was so kind that the animals were not afraid of her, and as for Rose Red—well, she was afraid of nothing.

Rose Red and her mother led a quiet life. In the summer Rose Red gathered roses from the rosebush  to decorate the table and mantel. In the winter she built a fire and put on the brass kettle that sparkled like gold. She would sit near the fire and listen to her mother read aloud from one of their many books.

One dark winter evening there came a loud thumping on the cottage door. Rose Red sprang up, thinking it must be a traveler seeking shelter from the cold. But when she unbolted the door, a great brown bear thrust his head in.

The poor widow screamed in terror.

Rose Red was not frightened. "May I help you, Mr. Bear?" she asked.

"I am half frozen and wish only to warm myself beside your fire," growled the bear through chattering teeth.

"Please come in and lie upon the hearth," said Rose Red, and she opened the door wide.

The bear stretched out wearily before the fire, while Rose Red fetched a broom. First she brushed the snow from his coat. Then she rubbed the bear with a towel until his fur was soft and gleaming. Before long Rose Red and the bear were tumbling and romping about the room like puppies. When it grew late, Rose Red fell fast asleep in her own bed, and the bear curled up by the fire.

Each morning Rose Red let the bear out of the cottage, and each evening he came back and lay down by the fire. Rose Red and her mother became so accustomed to him that the door was never bolted at night until he had arrived.

As soon as the last of the snow had melted, the bear said to Rose Red, "I must leave you now. I will not come again until autumn."

"But why must you go?" asked Rose Red.

"I have to search the forest for the wicked dwarf who stole my three treasures: a jar of pearls, a bag of coins, and a chest of jewels. All winter long he was trapped in his den beneath the snow, but now the ground has thawed and he is once again free."

Sadly, Rose Red opened the door to let the bear out one last time. As he left, his fur caught on the latch, and Rose Red saw a glint of gold underneath. But before she could say anything, the bear had disappeared into the forest.

ne morning not long after the bear's departure, Rose Red went to gather kindling for the fire. Walking along the forest path, she came upon a great oak tree that had fallen over. Crouched atop it was a tiny man with such wild hair that Rose Red could hardly see his face.

"What's the matter, sir?" asked Rose Red.

"You silly, stupid child!" screamed the little man. "Obviously I was trying to split this tree into firewood when my beautiful beard got caught." And indeed, Rose Red could now see that the end of his long beard was wedged deep in a cleft in the tree. She also noticed—for she had sharp eyes—that behind the fallen tree was a jar of pearls.

"Don't just stand there gawking at me!" shouted the little man, shaking his fists at her. "Can't you see I need your help?"

Now, Rose Red was a good-natured child, and of course she planned to help the dwarf. But she was also an intelligent child, and she realized that this rude little man was the very same dwarf who had stolen the bear's treasure. So she said, "I'd be happy to help you, sir, but I must ask you for that jar of pearls in return."

The dwarf shrieked with rage, but he told Rose Red she could have the pearls. Then Rose Red took a pair of scissors from her apron pocket and trimmed off the dwarf's beard.

"You've destroyed my beautiful beard, you wretched child!" screeched the dwarf. With that he vanished into the thicket.

Rose Red carried the jar of pearls home and put it on the mantel, to await the bear's arrival in autumn.

Three weeks later Rose Red set out for the town at the edge of the forest to buy some lace and ribbons for her mother. While walking home, she noticed an eagle had come to rest behind a large rock nearby.

Suddenly Rose Red heard a terrible scream. She ran to the rock just in time to see the eagle grab a large hairy bundle with its claws. It was the dwarf! Rose Red quickly grabbed the dwarf's legs before the great bird could carry him away. But though she struggled long and hard, she could not free the dwarf. The eagle's talons were tangled in his long, wild hair.

"Are you trying to save me or tear me in two?" screeched the dwarf, thrashing out with his arms. At that moment a bag filled with gold coins fell off his belt.

"I will save you," said Rose Red, knowing the coins belonged to the bear. "But first I must ask for those coins in return."

After much wailing the dwarf finally agreed. Rose Red took the scissors from her pocket and cut off the dwarf's wild hair. The eagle soared away.

"You've destroyed my beautiful hair!" screamed the dwarf, and with that he vanished behind some stones.

Rose Red carried the bag of coins home and put them on the mantel, next to the jar of pearls.

Another three weeks had passed by when Rose Red set out to catch some fish for supper. As she neared the stream, she found the dwarf thrashing around among the rushes.

"If you're not careful, sir, you will fall into the water," said Rose Red.

"Don't be ridiculous!" shrieked the dwarf. "Can't you see my handsome mustache has become tangled in my fishing line? Don't just stand there like a half-wit! Save me before I drown!"

 By this time Rose Red was quite used to the dwarf and looked around for the stolen treasure. And sure enough, hidden among the cattails, there stood the bear's chest of jewels.

"I'd be happy to, sir," replied Rose Red. "But I must ask you for that chest over there in return."

"Haven't I suffered enough?" screamed the dwarf. But he agreed, and Rose Red took out her scissors and carefully snipped off the dwarf's long mustache.

"Look what you've done!" screamed the dwarf.  "You've destroyed my handsome mustache!" Then, catching sight of his face reflected in the water, he let out an ear-piercing scream and vanished into the rushes. He was never seen again. You see, the dwarf's wicked power was in his hair, and without it he was just a miserable, ugly little man.

ust then Rose Red heard a noise behind her. She turned to see a great brown bear pushing through the bushes toward her. At each step bits of fur caught on the branches, revealing larger and larger patches of gold. As the bear came quite close, the last of his fur slipped away. There stood a handsome young man in a splendid gold costume.

"I am the son of a king," said the bear prince in a deep voice that sounded almost like a growl. "That dwarf stole my three treasures and put a spell on me to roam the forest as a wild beast. You have rescued my treasure and destroyed the dwarf's power. The spell is now broken, and I thank you."

Rose Red wasn't sure at first what to make of this stranger. But looking deep into his eyes, she recognized the bear. "You're welcome," she said.

Rose Red and the bear prince became the best of friends and spent many hours in each other's company. In time they fell in love and were married. Rose Red moved to the castle to live with her husband. As for the widow, she also came to live in the castle, and she brought with her the beautiful  rosebush. Rose Red and the bear prince planted it outside their window, and every year it bore the finest red roses in the land.

The End